D1292225

DISPOSSESSED

DISPOSSESSED

Philip Hodgins

Angus&Robertson
An imprint of HarperCollins*Publishers*

Publication of this title was assisted
by the Commonwealth Government
through the Australia Council,
its arts funding and advisory body.

An Angus & Robertson Publication

Angus&Robertson, an imprint of
HarperCollins*Publishers*
25 Ryde Road, Pymble, Sydney, NSW 2073, Australia
31 View Road, Glenfield, Auckland 10, New Zealand

First published by Angus & Robertson Publishers, Australia, 1994

Copyright © Philip Hodgins 1994
© Introduction – Robert Gray

This book is copyright.
Apart from any fair dealing for the purposes of private study,
research, criticism or review, as permitted under the Copyright Act,
no part may be reproduced by any process without written
permission. Inquiries should be addressed to the publishers.

National Library of Australia
Cataloguing-in-Publication data:

Hodgins, Philip, 1959-
Dispossessed.
ISBN 0 207 18294 9
I. Australia - Rural conditions - Poetry. I. Title.

A821.3

Cover painting by Bruce Howlett
Cover design by Robyn Latimer
Printed by McPherson's Printing Group, Victoria

9 8 7 6 5 4 3 2 1
97 96 95 94

Philip Hodgins was born in 1959, and lives in country Victoria. His work has been widely published in Australia and has appeared in journals in Europe, the UK, Asia and North America, including *Verse, The Times Literary Supplement* and *The New Yorker*.

He is married with two children.

By the Same Author

Blood and Bone
Down the Lake with Half a Chook
Animal Warmth
The End of the Season
Up on All Fours

ACKNOWLEDGEMENTS

Some of the chapters in this book originally appeared in the following publications: *The Adelaide Review; Antipodes* (USA); *Island Magazine* and *Quadrant*.

I would like to thank the Literature Board of the Australia Council for a one year Category A Fellowship, which enabled me to write this book.

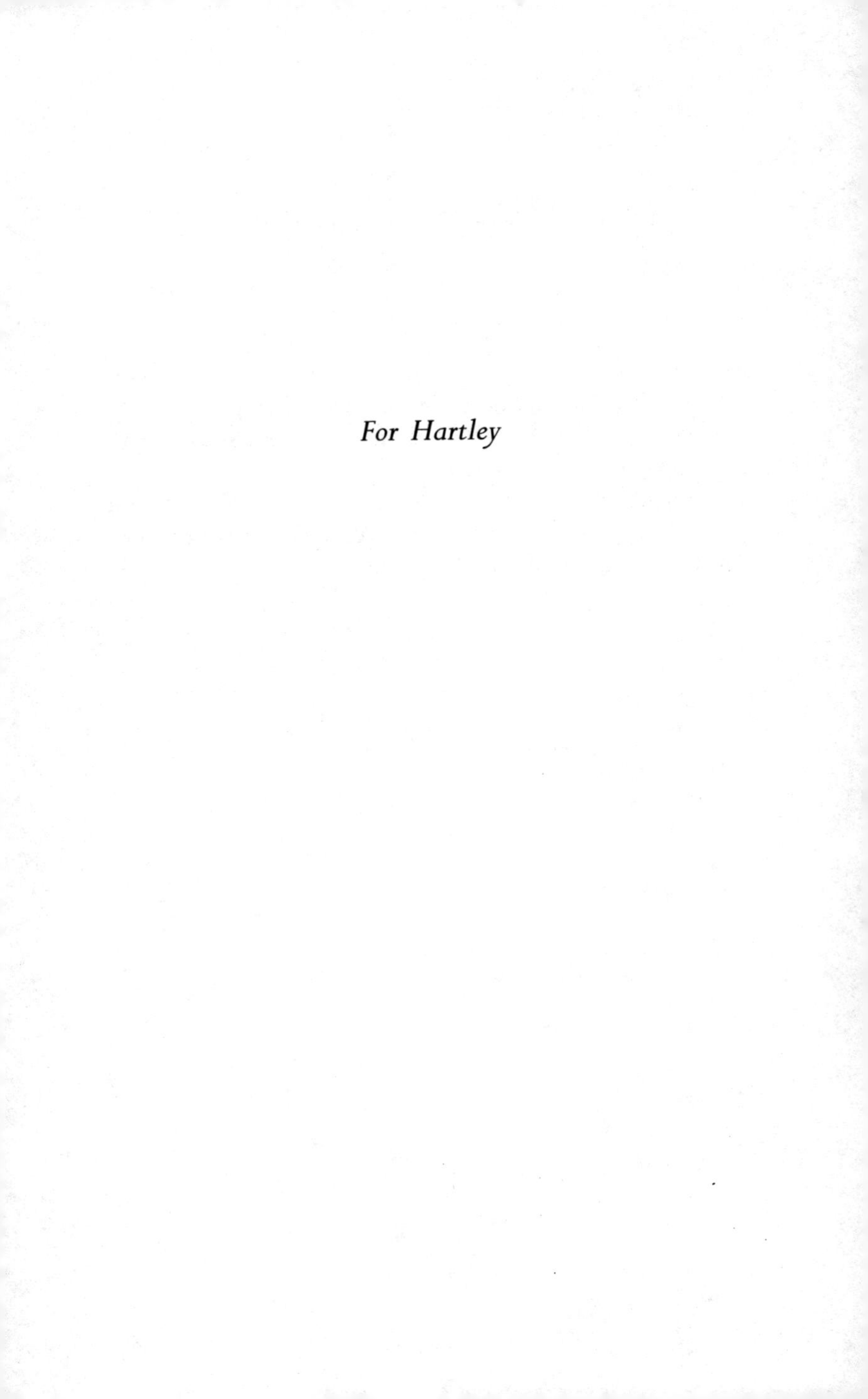

For Hartley

Introduction

Philip Hodgins is a younger writer who has already made a unique place for himself in Australian poetry, with his anti-Romantic, unwavering depictions of the reality of farming life in this country. Here, in *Dispossessed*, his verse novella, the reader is more than ever conscious of the contrasting subtlety, understatement, and suggestion in the way that he handles this theme. *Dispossessed* is told in the laconic and brutally unillusioned style of a rural anecdote, but in its form and its perceptions it shows a high level of sophistication.

The reader's tense presentiments, in the situation Hodgins creates here, turn out to be exactly those of the woman at the centre of the story — a development that is revealed with absolute concision. A further light touch and a rightness of observation are shown in the portrait of the child in her relations with her father. And the story's end, about the old man alone with his demons, is particularly striking in its economy and understanding.

Hodgins' narrative is full of ironies — overt ones, such as its being set in the year of the Bicentenary; or subtle ones, like a passing derogatory remark about the Aboriginals, which reveals a self-defeating lack of fellow-feeling in the marginalised white farmers.

Blank verse, one of our great cultural inheritances, could hardly have been more ironically used, one might think, than in treating these blank, unpoetic lives, and yet it is perfectly adapted here to carry the revealing, implicated rhythms of Australian speech. This book is another example of how poetry, with its concentration and its unmatched resources, is continuing to flourish and to retake its old areas of expression, in the modern world.

Dispossessed is about crudity, blunted feelings, burned-out emotions — things inseparable, it is suggested, from the way of life shown — but the subject is treated with an extraordinary artistic tact and discrimination.

ROBERT GRAY

CHAPTER ONE

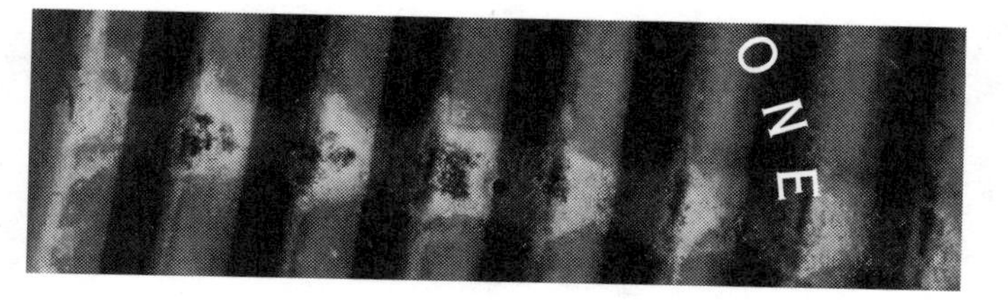

'Let's have a bit of light round here', said Len.
At first Amanda couldn't figure out
exactly what her father had in mind.
It was a moon-lit night. She stood there like
a child just taken from a burning house:
bare feet, bright red pyjamas underneath
a hurried dressing gown, and tapered lengths
of hair escaping from her bedtime plait.
Then she remembered what was in her hand:
the torch. She pressed it on and let the beam
float up into her father's face. 'Not me,
the bloody waterbag!' it squinted back.
Between them lay a groaning Friesian cow,
her head turned back as far as it would go
as if she were afraid of being attacked
by something from behind. Amanda poked
the torchlight down towards that area
and saw inside the blurry waterbag,
just where it poured unmoved out of the cow,
a pair of little ivory cloven hooves.
Her first impression was they looked like teeth.
'Yep. Good. You stay beside her mate', said Len
and headed for the far machinery shed,
his sloppy rubber boots producing one
more rhythmic sound to go with what was there:
the paddocks near them full of throbbing frogs,

DISPOSSESSED

the distant drumming of the poultry farm's
big generator left on overnight,
and Beris making long low *bhurr*, *bhurr*, *bhurrs*.
The moon was nearly full. Amanda stared.
She knew that if you looked for long enough
you'd see that it had moved. Sometimes in school
she'd watch the clock until the minute hand
had changed position on the big white face.
But movement from the moon was trickier.
You needed something to compare it with—
if possible the branches of a tree,
or even fingers held in a salute.
She noticed how one side, the left hand side,
was bulging slightly further than the right
by just enough to make a difference,
and it reminded her how it had been
the same with Beris for the last few weeks,
the right hand flank just bigger than the left.
She'd asked her Grandad, Len's Dad, what it meant
but all he'd said was that he wasn't sure,
most cows in calf were not quite uniform.
She watched her Dad returning from the shed.
His lanky frame assumed a hunchback shape
that soon turned out to be a coil of rope
through which a head and shoulder now emerged.
He put the rope down near the swollen cow

and slapped her rump until she straightened out
and stood up slowly with a heavy lurch,
the groans becoming louder as she did.
'You bring the rope. And where's yer boots?'
  said Len,
and started Beris off towards the big
old yellow-box that stood beside the fence.
Amanda made a proud decision not
to go inside and get her rubber boots,
deciding that her father would forget.
Her feet were aching on the cold wet grass
but she was eager not to miss a thing.
All through the week she'd been reminding Len
he'd promised that he'd get her out of bed
if Beris started calving in the night.
She noticed Miff, their cat, was following
a few yards further back, advancing through
the pasture with a kind of springy trot
and every now and then a high-curved leap,
which seemed to be for getting over some
fraught obstacle that only cats could see.
The mixed procession moved expandingly
and then contractingly towards the tree
so when they did arrive the order was
reversed, with Miff in front, Amanda next,
then Len preceding Beris backwards with

a thumb and finger through her slippery nose.
When they were near enough he stopped and nudged
her round so that her rear-end faced the tree.
He was about to ask again for light
when it appeared just where he wanted it.
'Good on ya mate', he said, and reaching out
he pinched the water bag so that it burst
and half a bucketful of amber slop
collapsed down Beris's back legs and went
beyond the circle of projected light.
It's horrible, Amanda knew at once.
Len pushed the sac up round the full smooth lips
and got his hand inside enough to tie
the greasy legs together to the rope.
Initially there was a sucking sound
and then it sounded like a stew being stirred.
While he was doing this Amanda saw
a nose being proffered on the outstretched legs.
He grabbed a section of the rope and tied
it round the flaky trunk at ringbark height,
and then he prodded Beris on the rump
so that she took a noisy forward step
which tightened up the rope to nearly straight.
He stood against the middle of this line
and with his wrists, elbows and shoulders pushed
a shallow springy vee each time there was

a *bhurr* from Beris at the other end.
Amanda watched him from behind and thought
it looked a bit like Mum when she was at
the kitchen table kneading dough for bread.
The rhythmic downward action was the same,
though this was slower and more serious.
She wondered if the torch were needed now,
decided that her father wouldn't care,
but left it turned on anyway to get
a better look at what was happening.
She noted its effect of switching on—
not only an intense display of centred light
but also, correspondingly, a more
intense excluded darkness all around.
The legs and half the head were out by now,
a brief gargoyle, and Len explained that once
the head and shoulders made it through the rest
would follow easily. So far the coat
was mostly black with just a single patch
of white below one knee. Another blob
appeared right on the forehead's bony peak
and when that part eventually squeezed out
the pained stretched skin surrounding it relaxed
a bit until the chest and shoulders forced
themselves into the middle of a ring
of opening flesh Amanda thought would split

it looked so pushed beyond its normal state.
Just then she noticed she was grimacing,
and tried to concentrate on being straight faced.
The birth was going as Len said it would.
Now that the widest parts were through he stepped
up closer to the cow and merely kept
his hand on Beris while the rest inched out.
What happened next reminded her of when
she'd seen a documentary on TV
with footage of the last few minutes of
a sinking ship. What seemed the same was how
a drawn-out process can accelerate.
The tapered calf was tilting further down.
It gathered speed and suddenly slid out
into the dark below her father's knees
and hit the ground with clumsy sodden weight.
Amanda's torch light quickly followed it.
'Too fast', said Len, and told Amanda how
he should have caught the calf before it fell,
or should at least have tried to slow it down.
'Looks like a girl', Amanda said. 'Yep. Girl!'
Len muttered, bending to his hands and knees,
and said he thought the calf would be all right.
He stuck his fingers down the rasping throat,
then wiped around inside the mouth, across
the nose, the eyes, and finally unblocked

the nostrils with a finger and a thumb.
While he was doing this Amanda felt
a kind of calmness coming over her.
Then it occurred to her it was because
the noise of Beris making all those *bhurr*s
had stopped. Instead she'd started going *mmm*
repeatedly, an even full bass sound
that resonated from her belly and
her throat, not very loud but still quite strong.
She now manoeuvred round to face the calf.
A length of afterbirth was hanging out
of her, just long enough to touch the ground,
and as she turned it wiped the dewy grass.
She nuzzled in, oblivious of Len,
and carefully began to lick the face
and forehead, smoothing tufts of pasted hair.
Len backed away and told Amanda how
the cow would lick the calf all over first,
and when the afterbirth had come right out
she'd probably eat part of that as well.
They stood there watching Beris for a while
and then he asked Amanda if she'd thought
about a name she'd like to give the calf.
'I reckon Jo's not bad', Amanda said.
'But that's a fella's name', said Len. 'Without
the *e*', replied Amanda, 'it's for girls'.

'Aaw yeah', said Len, remembering a name
from primary school. 'All right, it's Jo.
Let's get some sleep.' They turned and headed back
towards the kitchen light, its almost blue
fluorescent glow so much less powerful than
the moon's. While Len was getting through the fence
Amanda looked back up and saw how far
the moon had been delivered through the sky—
a greater distance than she would have guessed.
They must have been there for at least an hour.
The final thing she saw before she left
the paddock was the cow and calf unmoved,
and Miff, who'd stayed behind them, putting out
a paw to touch the draping afterbirth.

CHAPTER TWO

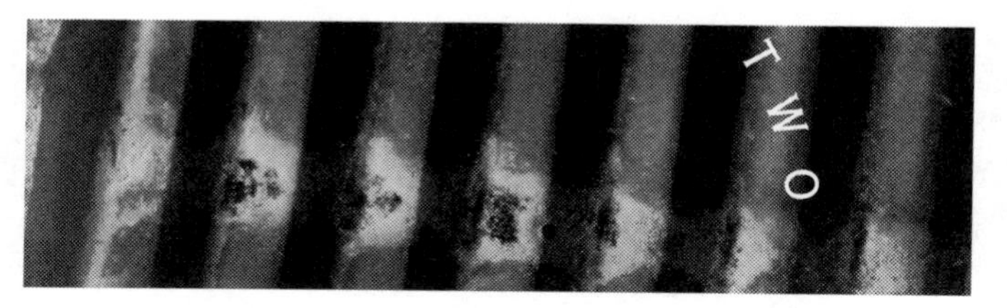

WHEN LIZ CAME IN AT EIGHT O'CLOCK SHE SAW
the big fluorescent light was still switched on,
from when the other two had got up in
the night to see the house cow calve, she guessed.
Bold sunlight was already tilting through
the eastern-facing window, bright enough
to kill off any challenge from the pair
of tubes clamped parallel at ceiling height,
the right one slightly stronger than the left;
and coming from a source above the tubes
were intermittent busy scratching sounds,
which Liz had noticed yesterday and that,
no doubt, were swallows nesting in the roof.
Her finger feeling for the switch, she looked
up at the pair of tubes so overwhelmed
by other light, and then she dropped her gaze
to table height where three raised pairs of eyes
were looking back at her. There was a click
and nothing changed. She put the kettle on
and sat down at the table. 'Afternoon',
said Max, his hands wrapped around a coffee mug.
'You bloody try being pregnant Pop', said Liz.
She got back up and stood beside the cracked
glass sliding door. The view was out across
the yard and into where the cow and calf
were standing now in gentle monochrome.

The calf was plugged into the left back teat,
her neck and head stretched down and front
  legs splayed
to make the soft connection possible.
Her tail was flicking unpredictably
and she was tugging at the teat so hard
you'd think that Beris would have kicked her off.
An area of afterbirth remained
and could be seen reflecting sunlight in
a gibbous pool not far behind the calf.
'Miff got another rabbit yesterday',
Amanda said. No one replied. She looked
at Len who looked away. 'I know', said Liz,
remembering the consequence: a pile
of sloppy vomit that she'd shovelled off
the doorstep with Amanda's plastic spade.
Miff often caught young rabbits in the spring.
She'd get them in the box-thorn down the creek
and almost always bring them to the house.
It was a mystery to Liz why Miff
would never learn to leave the pelt alone—
the fur was obviously what made her sick.
Most times the way it happened was the same.
She'd turn up with the rabbit in her mouth,
her head held high to keep it off the ground,
and settle on the doorstep for a play.

For half an hour or so the carcass would
be bitten, scratched, ignored, then pounced back on
until the bites became methodical.
The feet and legs were first to go, and then
the head, in pieces, followed by the moist
descent right through the body, peeling back
the flea-infested pelt in stages as
the flesh and bones and guts were burrowed out.
When Liz was watching through the sliding glass
she'd feel like intervening at this point
and taking what was left, the pelt, away.
But then she'd stop herself. Why interfere?
Miff never ate the pelt immediately.
She'd lie beside it with her eyes half-closed,
her belly almost big as pregnancy,
and stay there keeping guard, unmoved, as if
she had to gather strength before she could
begin to lick and tear off chewy tufts.
She would continue at it doggedly
until the final piece had been forced down
and only tiny drifts of fur remained,
and then there'd be a careless sniff at these
before she wandered off towards her spot
down by the willow tree beside the dam
or secret other places more remote.
When it was time to vomit she'd return.

Some instinct marked the doorstep as the place
this vulgar function had to be performed.
She'd arch her back and give a choking shake
and spew the rabbit out, converted to
a badly patterned pile of leaking lumps.
Occasionally she'd eat a few of these
again but mostly she'd just walk away,
no wiser than the last time this was done.
Liz crossed her arms. She'd woken feeling sick.
At seven months you'd think it should have passed
but something in this pregnancy felt wrong,
as if her body didn't want to have
another curled-up passenger inside
so many cycles since Amanda's time.
It must have been too much of a surprise,
thought Liz, half-jokingly. She'd given up
on having any other kids with Len.
They'd somehow had Amanda early on
and then no hint of action after that
until this one. She felt like vomiting.
She lit a cigarette. It didn't help.
As if it were a signal, Len and Max
both reached for cigarettes as well.
'Supposed to rain in Melbourne later on',
said Liz. 'You should have had those wipers fixed.'
No one replied. A thin high sound began.

The kettle boiled and blew its whistle off
into the gap between the gas rings where
the blackened griller was. It lay there for
a second dripping former steam until
Liz slightly burnt her thumb extracting it.
She made some instant coffee in a mug
and, looking over to Amanda, said
'You'll miss the bus'. 'We'll drop her there',
said Len.
There was a further stretch of silence while
the cigarettes and coffee were consumed.
Amanda doodled with a crust of toast.
The first to move was Len. 'You ready, Dad?'
he mumbled, briskly getting to his feet.
There was an ugly little noise from Max,
a combination of a cough and grunt,
while he obeyed his son's implied command
and slowly straightened upwards from the chair,
his hands remaining on the table top,
his jaw bone sticking out aggressively
as if he were about to make a speech.
Instead he left the room without a word.
'So what's it gonna be this time?' asked Liz.
'Down there? I wouldn't have a clue', said Len
Liz stared at him. 'Why go at all?' she asked.
'Well what the fuck are we supposed to do?'

he snapped. Liz looked away. He tried again:
'They mightn't wanna turf us out so soon'.
'Yeah, sure', she said. Amanda followed Len
outside where Max was sitting in the ute.
Liz stood back up beside the sliding door.
There were a few half-hearted waves, no smiles,
and then the ute took off across the yard.
Heard through the glass the tyres on gravel made
a sound like steady rain beginning on
the house's corrugated iron roof.
Liz fixed herself another coffee in
the mug she'd used before and sat down at
the table at the spot where Max had been.
She concentrated on the sounds the birds
were making in the roof. If anything
they seemed more agitated now, as though
a disagreement might be taking place.
She looked again to where she thought they were.
The scratching sounds were overtaken by
the sort of lightweight flurry small birds make
when they've been put inside a cardboard box.
These noises stopped when Liz half saw a pair
of swallows flitting out below the eaves,
their curved-back wings suggesting clever speed.
She settled down, enjoying being alone,
and thought of baking something in the range,

a cake or maybe bread while there was time,
and then decided she'd prefer to rest.
The thought of being evicted in a month
as well as almost constant nausea
had finally finished off the keenness Liz
once had to go that extra few per cent
(a favourite phrase of Len's) and make things nice.
She thought about herself ten years ago
when she and Len returned from Adelaide
to live across the road with Nan and Pop,
how much she'd tried to make things nice back then
by always baking bread and cakes and scones—
the hardest part was chopping all that wood
for Nan's old inefficient wood-fire stove—
and even afterwards when she and Len
had moved in here, how she'd still kept it up.
'Enthusiasm is a hardy plant.'
That Christian-sounding quote had surfaced in
her consciousness a few times recently.
She wondered where she'd first encountered it—
at either Sunday School or Church no doubt.
The image of her parents placing notes
of money into the collection bowl
week after week came sharply back to her.
The silver bowl was large and resonant.
It seemed designed to make the sound of coins

embarrassing, a clinking pettiness.
Her parents always paid in quiet notes.
How much would they have given in their life?
A bloody lot. And what a bloody waste.
One month of it would really help here now.
There wasn't any money in the house,
not one loose cent. They had to wait for Max
to dole them out a bit on shopping days.
How much did he have hidden over there?
Liz wondered if it might have been a lot
but then admitted that it couldn't be
or else they wouldn't be in such deep shit.
The swallows came back, bobbing past the eaves,
and disappeared into the ceiling where
the energetic sounds began again.
Outside, the lowered rigid shape of Miff
was easing through the grass towards a pair
of Red-Rumped Parrots picking at the ground
beside the barn where grain was sometimes spilled.
Liz watched, and kept on puzzling over Max.
Why wouldn't he allow them to apply
for all that stuff they were entitled to?
'Household Support' and 'Re-establishment'.
He said he couldn't stand the government
so why not make some use of it at least?
She knew what Max would say if he were asked.

'I've bloody worked for everything I've got',
or some such crap. But there was more to it,
she felt, than being too proud for charity.
It was a way for him to punish them,
especially Len, for losing everything:
for offering too much to get this place
and borrowing too much on what they had,
and worst of all to Max, for letting Len
convince him that the old place would be safe
to put up as the Mortgage Guarantee.
There was a burst of movement near the barn
as Miff accelerated from the grass
across the last few yards of open ground
exactly at the moment when the pair
of startled parrots flashed away from her.
As if to compensate for being too slow
she pounced on where they'd been and rolled around
before departing at a graceless trot.
Liz found herself remembering how Max
had seemed to her the first time that they met,
a harmless looking relic from the bush.
The fact that Liz had just been burgled in
her flat was mentioned early on by Len.
Instead of offering his sympathy
or asking what had gone, the older man
told Len to 'loan the girl some rabbit traps'

for when the flat would be unoccupied.
At first Liz thought he meant it as a joke
but then he went on to instruct her where
they should be set: in cupboards, boxes, drawers
and other places people put their hands.
It was the first of many times that Max
surprised her with the way he viewed the world.
She looked around at what was Len's world-view,
a pin-board nailed above the telephone,
that was his favoured filing cabinet.
The board itself was hardly visible
so many bits of paper covered it.
A lot of these were also covered up
by new editions of the same demand.
In several instances the same demand
was colour coded; so it might begin
as inoffensive as a royal blue,
become a pink Reminder in a month,
then finish up as serious as red.
But like a lot of things, the worst demands
looked quite subdued: small type, no colours, no
repeats. Liz looked at these: the letters from
the bank; the Notices to 'Pay' and 'Quit'
and photocopies of an Order of,
and Warrant of, 'Possession' from the Court.
This thought reminded her of something else,

a standing joke about Akubra hats—
the bigger be the brim, the smaller be
the farm (or variations on that line).
She looked a moment longer at the board,
reflecting on why Len preferred to stick
the evidence of his mistakes up there
where everyone would see it all the time,
but then forgot about it when she felt
a rolling movement in her swollen womb.
She opened several buttons on her shirt
and, drawing back the fabric, lightly pressed
her thumbs into the warm curved skin as if
examining a loaf of something she'd
just baked. The baby moved again. This time
it felt more like the little kick they'd seen
him make at four months on the ultrasound.
Len seemed delighted at the time and said:
'I bet he's gonna play for Collingwood!'
The ultrasound had been a good idea,
thought Liz, you knew what sex the baby was.
The photograph, in black and white, which they'd
been given afterwards was sticky-taped
above the mantelpiece. The image was
at first a sweeping blur, some random shapes
unfocused and at different distances
glimpsed through a windscreen on a wet dark night.

But then it changed the way Gestalt tests did
and what you saw made sense: an arm, a leg,
a bloated belly and a big-eyed skull.
She did her buttons up and thought about
arrangements for the birth, remembering
Amanda's thirty-three-hour coming out,
the way the pain was worse than anything
she'd ever known but that it somehow seemed
quite reasonable, and what a luxury
the next three days and nights in hospital
had been, no meals to cook, and lots of sleep
and healing baths between each feeding time,
and what a let-down coming home had been,
how Nan had disagreed about the name,
how Len had said he'd rather have a boy.

CHAPTER THREE

'A FUCKIN' LAZY BITCH, THAT'S WHAT SHE IS!'
No matter how much Len defended Liz
his father always seemed prepared to come
back with an even more aggressive line.
Len looked away to think of a reply
but then decided that he'd had enough
and concentrated on the paddock to
his left where near a silver dam a girl
about Amanda's age was walking towards
a pony with a halter hidden in
her hand behind her back. Her other hand
was holding out a tiny pile of grain.
Len watched until some trees broke up his view.
He was pissed-off. He'd had rebukes all day.
Max wouldn't even let him drive the ute.
He had to sit there like a twelve-year-old.
Between his feet there was a rubber mat
concealing several palm-sized holes where rust
had eaten through the floor. Len got a boot
toe underneath the mat and lifted it
away, allowing more road noises in.
He sat there for a minute looking through
the holes. That close the Calder Highway was
a fast smooth grey, reminding Len of fast
wide belts he used to see on old machines.
Aware that Max was giving him a look,

he let the mat drop limply into place
and stared back out the window to his left.
They both sat quiet for an hour or so
until a giant yellow sign loomed up
explaining that this section of the road
was being divided and upgraded as
a Project of the Bicentenary.
It triggered off a set response in Max
who went from total silence to a loud
long diatribe against the government
and in particular against Bob Hawke.
Len listened vaguely as he always did.
He knew what really irritated Max
was not the arrogance or money down
the drain or flogging off the farm to Japs
but that these people hadn't ever worked—
real work that is, by working with their hands.
He listened to a line he knew by heart,
how Hawke had made a living from his mouth,
and then he lost his concentration for
a minute while a semi-trailer packed
with cattle overtook them on the right.
He got back on the trail of words as Max
was saying Canberra was a shit-hole where
the biggest turds had floated to the top.
Receiving no encouragement, Max paused,

produced a few more metaphors, then stopped.
Len drifted into thoughts of documents
and what the Sheriff's Officer had said.
Max spoke again a few miles later on
as they were turning off the Calder near
Wahroonga Stud, a way home Len had not
been on for years. 'You got a smoke?' 'Run out',
lied Len. As if this were a challenge, Max
went through the pockets of his coat then scooped
around inside the glove box where he grabbed
a square tobacco tin, with flecks of rust,
tobacco-coloured, breaking up the shine.
He found there was about a teaspoon's worth
of dregs still left, along with several curled
old papers slightly stuck together by
their lines of gum. He peeled one off and pressed
it to the middle of his bottom lip
while at the same time slouching back so both
his knees came up against the steering wheel.
This freed his hands to roll the cigarette
but meant he couldn't see the road as well,
a change that didn't seem to bother him.
He filled the wetted paper with the dregs
and rolled and sealed it, steering with his knees
and raising frequent glances to the road.
For Len the choice was whether he should risk

a telling-off from Max and reach across
and hold the steering wheel more steadily
than Max's knees or whether he should just
ignore his father's carelessness. He looked
away, deciding to remain aloof.
He knew that Max would welcome any chance
to let him know that he'd been 'driving twice
as long as you have boy, and haven't had
a bingle yet'. He'd heard it all before.
They passed a lucerne paddock on the left
where sealed inside a tractor cabin with
his hat still on a man was mowing hay.
Len watched the low-slung mower slicing down
the crowded stalks. He wasn't near enough
to get a look at what was happening
but from the times he'd cut a crop like that
he could imagine clearly how it was,
how coming up against the sliding blades,
the stalks would seem to tremble, tip-toe, tilt
then throw themselves prostrate behind the line,
how perfumes of cut lucerne would be mixed
with diesel perfumes if the air was still,
and how the forceful low-down tractor sounds
would go on like a mantra meaning *work*.
The man had nearly finished with this cut.
He'd worked his way into the centre of

the paddock where a green dense-looking square,
no more than fifty feet across, was left
still standing like some kind of fortress where
the countryside all round had been laid waste.
The scene reminded Len of years ago
when he was nine or ten. He'd been with Max
all day up on the tractor cutting hay.
They'd mowed the paddock to a square just like
the one they now were passing on the left:
a few more minutes' work would bring it down.
His father told him how you often get
a bit of wildlife in the last few rows.
If something's in the crop, the circling noise
will drive it inwards to the centre
of a disappearing world. With several rows
to go, the riders looked behind and saw
a rabbit hopping hopelessly away.
When Len jumped down and picked it up he found
the back feet mutilated by the blades.
The thing that he remembered most was how
it left a bloody pattern on his hands
when Max had taken it away from him
and smashed its head against the engine block.
Len twisted round to watch the paddock slide
into the past to join that other one,
reflecting that he was an adult now

but that the situation hadn't changed,
his father still sat in the driver's seat.
The ute went down a slope towards a creek.
It gave the occupants a moment free
of sunlight in their eyes. They crossed a bridge
just as the narrow road swung back to flat.
Beside the bridge a sign said POISON CREEK.
'They shoulda fuckin' got 'em all', said Max.
Len went to speak then closed his mouth again.
He felt he was expected to agree
but couldn't figure out what Max had meant.
He sat there with a slightly furrowed brow,
his head tipped down to see the other sign
receding in the mirror on his side.
The bridge was out of sight before he twigged:
an incident, last century no doubt.
It only showed what he already knew:
his father had a kind of mental map
of all this country round the centre of
the state, a chart of folklore, anecdote
and rumour, which he used to read the land.
He thought about some places nearer home,
considered asking Max about a name
he'd always thought was odd, but dropped it when
his father switched the wireless on too loud.
The sun was almost sitting on the road

ahead of them, like some apocalypse
they'd soon be coming to. It wasn't safe
to drive directly at a sun so low,
thought Len, but didn't think of telling Max.
He knew his father wouldn't stop and wait.
He looked across and saw a screwed-up face,
the eyes reduced to soft defensive slits,
the hand that rested on the steering wheel
held up as if it could deter the sun.
His father's stubbornness, together with
the stifling sunlight and the wireless noise,
was suddenly too much for Len to bear.
He went through reasons he could use to stop
and figured asking for a piss was best—
he could have done with one soon anyway.
But while he thought about it things improved:
the road merged left into a wider one,
which Len then recognised as only half
an hour from home, and at the same time Max
turned off the wireless with a left-hand jab.
Without the interfering noise and light,
the cabin atmosphere was not so bad
and Len decided he could stick it out.
The sun had gone when they arrived back home
but there was light enough to make the trees
along the creek a ragged silhouette,

a narrow dark torn strip laid out between
the new growth paddocks and the polished sky.
The ute slowed down for Len to clamber out,
then kept on going to the other place.
Len paused a minute in the yard and ran
his eyes along the treeline, thinking back
on something Liz had pointed out to him,
how no new trees were coming on down there
because of years and years of grazing stock.
Each spring the seedlings would be bitten off.
And when those stands of big old trees had died,
who knows, erosion and salinity?
Suppose it's not our problem now, thought Len.
He almost smiled remembering how Max
had sneered when Liz had mentioned it to him.
He reckoned it was crap. No wonder he
refused to join the local landcare group.
His mind was closed. He didn't even think
the Yanks had landed on the moon back then.
He reckoned it was all a TV show,
a big production out of Hollywood.
Len turned and walked towards the sliding door
where Liz was standing inside watching him.
'So what was keeping you out there?' asked Liz.
'Just thinking what a prick the old man is',
he said. 'I coulda told you that ten years

ago', she said. 'What happened with the date?'
'No bloody good. There's nothing we can do.'
He took a folded piece of paper from
his pocket, opened it, then pinned it on
the crowded board above the telephone.
Liz saw it was the Sheriff's letterhead.
She peered at it and said, 'Those noises in
the roof were swallows. Got a look at 'em
this morning. Guess they must be nesting there'.
'They're mad', said Len, 'the rats'll get the eggs'.
He lit a cigarette, inhaled, then placed
it in an ashtray on the table while
he took his jumper off aggressively
like someone getting ready for a fight.
'You fed the dogs?' he asked. 'Just going now',
said Liz. 'That fella with the funny name
came back.' She stepped in front of Len and grabbed
an open bag of pellets off the bench,
pulled back the sliding door and went outside.
Len took his cigarette and followed her.
The outside air was still and smelled of hay.
He closed the door and stood there watching Liz
who faded to the far side of the yard.
His lungs filled up with smoke, he held his breath
and listened as the chains spilled out of two
tipped-over forty-fours, a ratchet sound

of metal knuckles tripping over lips
of metal, followed by the jackpot sound
of pellets poured into a metal dish.

CHAPTER FOUR

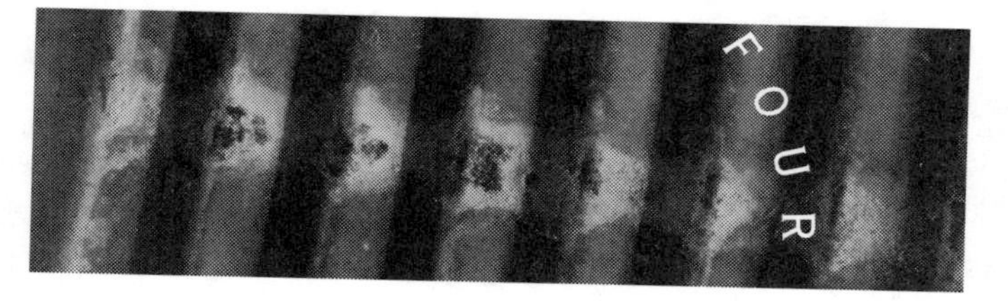

'SURRENDERED DEAR! WITHOUT A SHOT!' SAID LIZ.
She stepped into the kitchen with a big
green cabbage in her hands. Amanda came
behind her, pulling shut the sliding door.
Len looked at what was on the kitchen bench:
a pair of rifles with the bolts removed,
a telescopic sight, two mounts, a file,
a magazine, and half a dozen screws.
And then he looked at what was in his hands:
a length of wire to which a small white rag
was tightly hooked. 'Hilarious', he said.
'This thing's as heavy as a cannon ball',
said Liz, depositing the cabbage in
the sink beside a pair of dirty mugs.
She filled the kettle, put it on and gave
the mugs a hurried rinse. 'What's this about?'
she asked, examining the arsenal.
'I'm gonna get some roo meat for the dogs',
he said. 'They haven't had fresh meat for weeks.'
'How legal's that?' asked Liz. Amanda found
a bullet on the table Len had missed
when he was sorting ammo earlier.
'Can I have this?' she asked. 'No bloody way',
said Len. 'It's dangerous.' He turned and took
a rifle off the bench, the bigger one,
a two-four-three, and held it to the light

and looked along inside the barrel where
the rifling ran in polished vertigo.
He couldn't see a single speck of dirt
but undeterred he fed the wire down through
the breech until a trembling tip came out
the muzzle, then he pulled the rest inside
so that the rag was momentarily
compressed into a long soft sliding plug.
He put the two-four-three back on the bench
then took the smaller one, a twenty-two,
and squinted through it like a telescope.
Again not seeing any dirt, he still
went through the business with the wire and rag.
He put the rifle back and went off to
another room in search of bullets for
the two-four-three. There was the random noise
of someone rummaging through sets of drawers
and then the boom you get from rolling shut
a filing cabinet with too much force.
Liz leaned against the table with her hands
joined underneath her heavy belly like
she'd had them round the cabbage earlier.
Amanda fiddled with her bullet while
she wondered if she'd be allowed to go
with Len despite her mother's views on guns.
The kettle started issuing a noise

like static from a distant radio.
When Len returned it had already boiled.
A pot of tea was sitting on the bench.
He dropped a box of bullets down beside
the pot. The cover said point two-four-three.
He opened it and absent-mindedly
began to take the bullets out and stand
them in a line: one, two, three, four, five, six,
like gleaming model soldiers on parade.
'How legal's what?' he said, as if he'd just
been asked the question Liz had put to him
before he'd checked the bores and left the room.
She looked at Len, but didn't answer him.
He smiled and said, 'I wouldn't break the law'.
'Oh yeah? Those guns aren't even registered!
I'll dob on ya!' she said, and walked across
to where he was and flicked a bullet so
the others toppled like five dominoes.
Len smiled again and said, 'It's fine. They're on
our land. The old man saw them yesterday
down past the paddock where the cattle are'.
Liz poured the tea into the pair of mugs
and said, 'You need a permit don't ya, though?'.
Len shook his head and then began to feed
the fallen bullets to the magazine.
Amanda watched them going in side-on,

their sloping shoulders and their pointy heads
associated in her mind with bangs
so loud they nearly knocked you off your feet.
The memory of hearing one explode
the first time Len had taken her to shoot
still bothered her. Her ears had rung for hours.
She squeezed the bullet that she'd found before,
a hollow-pointed twenty-two, now warm
and sweaty from ten minutes in her hands,
and thought how quiet, small and blunt it was
compared with those big brutes. She watched as Len
snapped in the bolts and magazine, picked up
the other stuff and headed for the door.
'I'm coming too', she said. Len paused as if
he might be listening to the swallows in
the roof. 'Why not? Good on ya, mate!' he said,
and stepped out over Miff who lay across
the doorstep watching sparrows on the lawn.
Amanda looked at Liz, expecting her
to say how careful you should be with guns
but all she said was 'Go and get some shoes'.
By sweeping underneath the table with
one straightened foot and leg in what was like
a ballet exercise, Amanda found
her sneakers with the socks tucked into them.
She quickly put them on and went outside

before Liz had a chance to change her mind.
At first Amanda headed for the ute,
but seeing it was empty, looked around
the yard until she saw her father in
the far machinery shed, hunched over where
she knew a vice was bolted to a bench.
Arriving there she found that Len had clamped
the two-four-three into the slow hard jaws
so that it pointed down the bench's length
towards the corrugated iron wall
about ten yards away. 'What's this?' she said.
'You'll see', said Len. He held the trigger down
and eased the silver bolt out of the breech
as gently as you might defuse a bomb
then wrapped it in his handkerchief and put
it on the window ledge above the bench.
To keep it free of dust, Amanda guessed.
The rifle in the vice began to look
familiar now. She paused, remembering
last year she'd come across a twenty-two
clamped in a vice in one of Max's sheds.
She'd meant to ask an adult at the time
what it was for but no-one was around.
Len took a box of matches off the bench
and set it on a noggin in the wall.
Returning to the gun, he peeped along

the bore. 'Not quite', he said, and trotted back
and moved the box a fraction to the left.
Then when he peered again into the breech
he murmured, 'Yep. Spot on'. Amanda stared,
suspecting he was going to shoot the box.
Instead, he swung a leg up on the bench
the way that snooker players sometimes do
and got his head right in behind the breech.
Absorbed in what was visible to him
he seemed almost as rigid as the gun,
and when he did relax his actions were
confined to minor movements of both hands:
the left one wrapped around the handle of
the vice, the right one resting on the butt.
He slowly gave the handle half a turn
and tapped a few times on the butt so that
the muzzle lifted imperceptibly.
'How long's this gonna take?' Amanda asked.
'Not long', said Len, and stood up straight again
and turned the handle back as far as it
would go. 'Just gotta do the sight', he said.
Amanda watched him fixing on the sight,
his fingers working automatically
like fingers do on a production line.
It's always longer than he says, she thought.
Len started on about trajectory

while he resumed his horizontal pose,
this time his eye hard in behind the sight.
He worked away, adjusting tiny screws
with cautious ever-smaller turns until
his fingers didn't seem to move at all.
'That's it', he said. 'You wanna have a squiz?'
Amanda balanced on a fruit case for
a better look. She peered along the bore.
The barrel's aim was just above the box.
She raised her head and stared into the sight.
The box was bigger now. Amanda frowned
to see the hair-lines cross exactly in
the centre of the famous Redhead's face.
'Hang on! How come they aren't the same?'
  she asked.
'Just what I said. Trajectory!' said Len.
They took their things and got into the ute.
Len wedged the rifles in behind the seat.
Amanda propped up on a cushion for
a better look. 'I'll do the gates', she said.
They set off down a gravel lane with Len
still going on about trajectory:
how wind resistance, gravity and spin
will all contribute to the bullet's path.
Amanda found it hard to concentrate.
A paddock gate went past them on the left.

It coincided with the start of splats
and dolloped shapes and wonky dotted lines
of recent cowshit patterning the lane.
Had Max just shifted cattle into there?
Or moved them out? Amanda wondered while
she listened to the rain beginning sound
of cowshit flicked up underneath the ute.
The further on they went, the less there was.
She guessed this meant the cattle there had gone
to join up with the main part of the herd.
The lane veered left and ended with a gate.
Amanda hurried from the ute, undid
the chain, put one foot on the gate and with
the other hopped and pushed herself along
like children do on scooters. 'Hey!' yelled Len.
'Get off the bloody gate! You'll make it drop.'
She looked the other way while Len drove through
then she returned the gate by shooing it
a few times with her hand the way you would
if you were herding something like a cow
or bull. The gate collided with its bolt.
There was a double clank accompanied by
a longer background note that sounded like
a damaged tuning fork. Amanda did
the chain and joined her father in the ute.
'Just gotta see the old man first', said Len.

He gave the steering wheel a clockwise turn,
accelerating as he did. A pack
of cigarettes went sliding off the dash.
'Owzat!?' appealed Amanda, catching them
before they hit the floor between her feet.
She saw that Max's truck was over where
the cattle were and hoped it wouldn't take
too long. When Len pulled up and walked across
to Max she stayed behind as if it might
encourage them to get their business done.
The engine idled unpredictably,
always about to stall. Amanda sat
and watched and wondered what was going on.
Len's dogs were running back and forth around
the sleek enormous herd of Herefords,
just managing to keep them in one shape
while Max and Len stood talking near the truck.
The cattle's creamy whites and outback reds
were constantly being moved and rearranged,
revolving on a shifting axis, which
was kept as far away as possible
from where the dogs were seen at any time.
The more you looked, the more confused you got.
Most of the time you couldn't say where one
cow stopped and where another one began.
The only ones you could be sure about

were those along the outside of the herd.
A lot of flanks had shit stain shapes on them
from being pressed up so close. Amanda watched
another tail lift out. This time the load
of dark green slop was poured into a face.
She wondered why so many noses trailed
a line or two of clear thin mucus in
the morning breeze and why so many big
strong cows seemed so afraid of two old dogs,
and then she yawned and concentrated on
the gauge that told the engine temperature.
Its little arm had nearly reached the top.
She reached across and tapped it lightly with
her fingernail so that it made a noise
like one she'd sometimes heard the swallows make.
Her interest disappeared as soon as Len
came back towards the ute. Hooray, she thought.
But all he did was reach into the dash
and switch the engine off, then walk head down
back over to the truck where Max was propped
against the grille about to role a smoke.
With both his hands together out in front
and shoulders hunching forward, he was in
a pose the same as one he'd used to show
Amanda how to take a chest mark when
they'd kicked the footy after school last week.

She watched the two men start to talk again.
They both made cranky gestures with their hands.
She waited for a minute, then wound down
the window on her side and yelled, 'Come on!'
Both Max and Len stopped talking, turned to look
with that annoyed expression that you get
from people who've just had a stranger barge
into their room, and then resumed their talk.
She watched them for a minute more before
experimenting with the radio,
investigating what the glove box held
and finally refocusing on what
the herd was doing now the dogs had gone
to lie like vagrants underneath the truck.
None of the cows was standing still but most
of them were slowing down. They seemed to wheel
off-centre, dragging to a massive halt.
Amanda watched a bull come muscling through
the herd until he reached the outside, stopped,
then forced his way back in. He had the air
of one who likes to throw his weight around.
She looked the other way and thought about
the moment's view she'd had of that thick frame,
how something in his shape was threatening.
His head was bigger than a cow's and had
more pits and lumpy areas, as if

a sculptor hadn't finished chiselling it.
The legs were short and thicker than a cow's
and up the front the chest was closer to
the ground and wider too. The shoulders were
enormous but the rear end tapered off
surprisingly so that the body from
the side was like a clumsy giant wedge.
His ball-bag hung down like a footy in
a big pink sock. It too was near the ground.
Amanda turned to look for him again
and saw that Len was walking to the ute.
He reached in first, took out the two-four-three,
slid in the magazine and hit it with
an open-handed uppercut then drew
the bolt and snapped the loaded chamber shut.
'You had an argument?' Amanda asked
as Len sat down. He shut the door so that
the barrel pointed out the window and
the butt was elevating from his lap.
'Aw yeah. Not one that matters much', he said.
They set off to the paddock further on
where Max had seen the roos. The gate was shut
but to its left there was a cattle grid.
Despite Len slowing down to cross the bars
there was a nasty burst of rapid thuds
that sounded like two boxers in a ring.

Len did a sharp right turn and drove along
the fenceline to the nearest corner where
about a dozen full-grown red-gums stood.
He stopped the ute and switched the engine off.
The space beneath the trees was taken up
almost entirely by a box-thorn mass.
Just like the cows, you couldn't tell where one
left off and where another one began.
There was a grassless area right round
the box-thorns, shot with rabbit holes, scratched loose
and dotted with the rabbits' dung, which had
a shotgun pellet uniformity.
'Don't s'pose you'd get a roo in there', said Len.
Amanda saw not far from where they were
a rabbit drooping in a myxo haze.
Its eyes were bloodshot and its fur was worn.
It seemed to sense that there was danger near
but couldn't get away. It tottered round
in hopeless circles for a bit then stopped.
'Shoot that!' Amanda said. 'No point', said Len.
They drove along the fence towards the creek.
Amanda scanned the paddock hoping she
could spot a roo before her father did,
but by the time they'd reached the creek she had
admitted to herself that there was none.
Len stopped and got out with the two-four-three.

He held it up, and looking through the sight
he swept from left to right examining
things on the edge of visibility
the way the captain of a sailing ship
might do. Amanda climbed out just in time
to see the level barrel sweeping past
her head the way a mainsail boom might do.
'No good', said Len. 'Might bring the spotlight back
tonight. Don't think they're still around here though.'
He climbed back in and took the handbrake off.
'We'll have a shot down where the slagheap is',
he added as the ute began to roll.
'Oh good!' Amanda said. They drove along
the creek in second gear, avoiding trees
but staying close enough to get a look.
The creek was pretty low. You couldn't see
it moving much except in places where
it narrowed and a rippling grid of spun
diagonals appeared. Or now and then
a fallen trunk or boulder half-submerged
would make the water rise and spread in curved
envelopment the way a submarine
bow looks before it's fully re-emerged.
Amanda looked across at Len. 'You know
the day we're s'posed to leave', she said. 'Do we
just have to get out, you know, when they say?'

'Something like that', said Len. 'But they can't force
us if we didn't wanna go', she said.
'They bloody wouldn't wanna try', said Len.
Amanda was about to speak again
when suddenly a Red-Necked Wallaby
was bounding frantically away from them.
They must have nearly run right over it.
'You friggin' ripper! You'll do me!' cried Len.
Before Amanda could collect her thoughts
the ute had skidded to a handbrake stop
and Len was leaning on his open door,
the two-four-three trained on the wallaby.
She just had time to close her eyes and put
her index fingers in her ears before
a stunning bang engulfed the cabin and
was gone. She looked at where the wallaby
had been. 'It got away!' she said. 'Did not!'
said Len. He took the handbrake off and drove
to where Amanda had been looking when
she closed her eyes. They found the carcass in
a small depression further on from there.
It had a groggy look fixed on its face,
a bloody patch below the auburn band
across its neck and shoulders, and a lot
of glossy blood all down its pallid chest.
'Right through the heart I'd say', said Len, his head

bowed down, his legs together and his hands
behind his back. He looked like someone at
a funeral standing by the open grave.
They stood there for a while as if they might
be paying last respects, then Len picked up
the tail and hauled the carcass over to
the ute. Amanda followed close behind,
amused at how the head was nodding as
it dragged across the contours of the ground.
Len stepped into the back and lifted in
the wallaby. 'Should keep 'em going for
a bit', he said. Keep what? Amanda thought,
and then remembered what the meat was for.
They got into the front and started off
in silence. Further down the line of trees
a mullock heap like some small pyramid
came into view. Amanda focused on
its peak, remembering the times she'd climbed
up there, how good the panorama was.
'Do many people lose their farms?' she asked.
'Yeah, always some', said Len. 'I tell ya what,
there's gonna be a whole lot more though. Stacks.
These feed-lots keep on springing up you won't
have any farmers left.' He shook his head
and looked out at the creek. Amanda turned
to ask him what a feed-lot was but stopped.

'They gotta lotta gold round here you know',
he said. How much is left? Amanda thought.
The mullock heap was mostly ecru clay,
sunbaked, with darker patches of what looked
like shale emerging low down on one side.
There was a scattering of rabbit holes
around but nothing on the heap itself.
A fair few beer cans lay around as well:
some new, some rusty, most with bullet holes.
Len gathered half a dozen up and stood
them on the ground a yard in front of where
the heap began to rise. The twenty-two
was just a single shot. He loaded it
and passed it to Amanda. 'Two bob
a hit!' he said She tried to get the front
and rear sights lined up with a can but found
the muzzle end was doodling constantly
in front of her. 'It weighs too much!' she said.
Receiving no encouragement from Len
she squeezed the trigger when she felt the sights
had wandered into line. The recoil and
the bang were not too bad. 'What happened?' asked
Amanda. 'You went over them', said Len.
'Start off too high then let it come down slow.'
He took a crumpled box of bullets from
a pocket of his coat. 'Last one!' he said.

'Should have a few more in the ute.' He took
the rifle from Amanda, loaded it
then gave it back. She aimed the thing above
the cans and found she could indeed control
its fall more easily than lifting it.
She fired again. This time the shot was low.
It hit the ground in front but skidded up
and caught a can as it went through. The can
spun backwards for about a foot then stopped.
'Good on ya mate!' said Len, and headed for
the ute. Amanda laid the rifle down
with care and ducked round to the far side of
the mullock heap, unzipped her jeans and had
a pee. On her way back she looked across
the paddocks to a silver square of light
reflecting from a roof, the galvo slopes
of home, and thought about the swallows there.
Len hadn't found the bullets. 'Shit' she heard
him say. She watched him rummaging as if
he had to find his licence for a cop.
A couple of galahs went overhead.
She reached into the pockets of her jeans,
expecting she'd still have the bullet that
she'd taken earlier, but it was gone.

CHAPTER FIVE

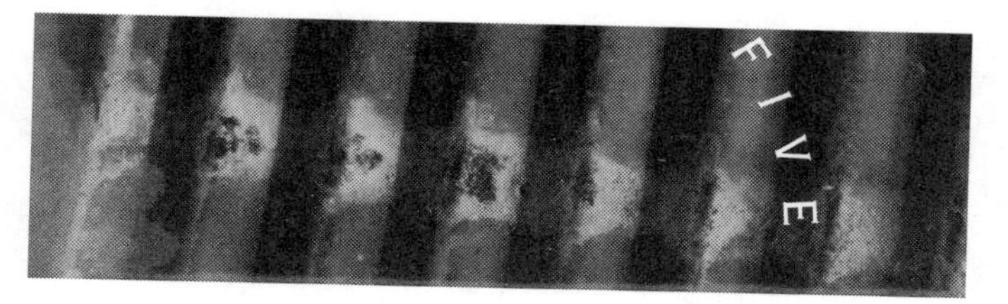

'DAD SAYS WE'RE GONNA SHOOT IT OUT! YOU KNOW,
the day we're s'posed to leave!' The sound of milk
syringing into Liz's bucket stopped.
And then resumed. She shifted on her stool,
a metal child-sized one with four thin legs
that splayed out like the calf at feeding time,
and tilted back her head so she could look
into her daughter's animated face.
Amanda had both hands around the straps
of Beris's loose halter, holding her
in place while Liz squeezed out the breathy milk.
'That's typical of something Len'd say',
said Liz, deciding half a bucketful
would do. She stood up with the bucket in
one hand, the stool a less than equal sort
of counterbalance in the other one.
'All right, we'll let that hungry calf in now',
she said, and headed with her load towards
the fence. Amanda ran the other way,
down to the corner of the paddock where
a little galvo shed was nestled like
a cubbyhouse. Its ancient wooden door
was bolted shut, but through the rails that formed
the partly open top half of its front
Jo's head was visible. She stuck her nose
out through the rails as far as it would go

and made an unattractive bleating noise.
Liz reached the fence and threw the stool across,
then swung the bucket over with more care.
A raindrop landed on her upturned cheek.
She pulled two middle wires apart and forced
herself between the bowed outline they formed.
I feel like Beris would if she tried this,
thought Liz, regaining equilibrium.
She looked in the direction of the shed,
expecting that Amanda would have let
the calf out now. Instead she saw the door
still shut and Jo's raised nose still poking through
the rails, Amanda's fingers in her mouth.
'Come on! That isn't fair!' yelled Liz. 'She wants
a drink.' Amanda took her fingers out
and wiped a slimy white froth on her jeans,
then slid the bolt and headed over to
the place where Liz had just climbed through
the fence.
At first the door stayed shut but then Jo's head
appeared, and swivelled like a side-show clown's.
This pushed the door enough to swing it back.
Jo trotted out, then seeing Beris charged
across the little paddock at full speed,
her tail held up so that the end of it
swung lazily the way a lasso does.

Arriving at the place her mother was,
she butted Beris's big udder like
a punching bag, then latched onto a teat.
She settled to a sucking rhythm, which
involved a lot of tugging and a lot
of shaking of her tail. 'She's pretty rough',
Amanda said. 'You were like that', said Liz.
They walked back to the house. Amanda made
a point of carrying the bucket for
her 'poor sick mother'. Can't be serious,
thought Liz. Amanda's method seemed odd too.
Instead of holding it one-handed at
her side, she held it with both hands in front,
chest-high, so she was looking through the arch
the handle formed, and so the milk slopped out
occasionally. Sometimes it wet her shirt
and other times it landed in the grass
where Miff, who had appeared, would stick her nose.
'You're making quite a meal of that you know',
said Liz. 'I gotta keep these animals
away', Amanda said. They crossed the lawn
and went into the kitchen where the smells
of coffee, toast and cigarettes were mixed.
'The milkman's here!' said Max. Amanda set
the bucket on the table. 'Wanna jug?'
asked Liz. 'Still got one from the other day',

he said. Amanda took some corn flakes from
a cupboard, opened them and filled a bowl.
She scooped some milk out of the bucket with
a mug and poured it in, then scattered two
teaspoons of caster sugar over them.
She found a spoon and took her first mouthful.
'Still warm', she smiled, and hurried several more.
'I've made two resolutions Pop', said Liz.
Max looked at her with eyebrows raised. 'The first
one is I'm gonna get more exercise.
The second is I'm gonna give the fags
away. Don't look at me like that!' she said.
'We've heard this sorta thing before', said Max.
'I'm serious. I'm sick of feeling sick.
I haven't had a decent walk for yonks.
I used to love a walk along the creek',
she said. 'Well, it's still there', said Max. He pulled
his left boot off and shook it upside-down.
A fair amount of yellow chaff fell out,
and something harder that you didn't see.
It bounced a few times on the floor before
the chaff arrived. 'Where's Dad?' Amanda asked.
'He's down the paddock. Wanna come?' said Max
Amanda looked across at Liz, who said,
'You better have a coat. It's gonna rain'.
Liz made herself a mug of coffee while

Amanda changed her shirt and shoes and found
her plastic coat. Max pulled his right boot off
and shook it like the other one. This time
he only got a scattering of chaff.
'I'll get the brush and pan for you', said Liz.
Max smiled. 'Floor's dirty anyway', he said.
Amanda came in with her raincoat on.
Max looked at her. 'They back to school next week?'
he asked. Liz nodded, 'Yep'. He stood up with
a cough and used the back of his left hand
to wipe his nose. 'All right, let's go', he said.
Amanda went out first, then Max, who stopped
framed in the open sliding door and said,
'Aw by the way I gave Len eighty quid'.
Liz nodded at him knowingly. She watched
them get into the truck and sit there while
its engine whined and whined but didn't catch.
The whining slowed, became a moan and stopped.
The bonnet popped and Max climbed out with tools
and what looked like some sort of aerosol.
He propped the bonnet, leaned half-in and yelled
instructions to Amanda while he worked.
She slid across to Max's side and reached
down with her feet as if she couldn't touch
the bottom of a swimming hole. 'Yeah, good!'
yelled Max. She bent forward and turned the key.

The engine fired almost immediately.
And then backfired and kept on going with
a pile of blue smoke building at the rear.
Max dropped the bonnet. 'Fucking bitch!' Liz heard
him yell. Amanda slid across again.
He got back in and drove the truck away.
Don't swear like that in front of her, thought Liz.
She drained her mug and set it on the sink
then ran her fingers slowly through her hair.
'Raincoat', she said, and went into the lounge,
put on an oilskin coat and went outside.
The sky was overcast. The clouds were thick.
The densest ones were over to the west
above the Pyrenees, a shadowed bank
of solid purple looking like a range
of mountains further back. The air had that
electric smell you sometimes get with rain.
Liz calculated that she had an hour
or so before the downpour would arrive.
She set off at an energetic walk,
remembering 'a good aerobics base'
and other phrases from her Phys. Ed. days.
Her pulse went up almost immediately.
My God, I must be so unfit, she thought.
Her breathing deepened and her hands grew tight
with extra blood. She squeezed them into fists.

The deeper breaths felt good. She held them in
and let them out deliberately as she'd
been taught to do when she was learning how
to meditate. Her teacher used to say
that this was how you reach your inner self.
The stuff you swallow when you're young,
  she thought.
She slowed her stride, deciding that she'd best
not overdo it with the extra weight.
Her nausea, surprisingly, was just
the same as if she had her feet up in
the house. I should do more of this, she thought,
it doesn't seem to make it any worse.
The gate across the track down to the creek
was open, so she sauntered through, relieved.
It was a heavy bastard since the end
had dropped—no doubt Amanda swinging there
had been the cause. You had to drag it like
a big unwieldy compass. Proof of this
was on the gravelly ground, a perfect arc
inscribed between the bolt post and the far
side of the track. A mile or so away,
in line with those big rain clouds to the west,
a flock of sulphur-crested cockatoos
was breaking up and eddying, and then
reforming so it could be done again.

The darkness of the clouds behind them made
their whiteness even brighter, so their wings
were almost flickering. Liz listened to
their raucous screeching, sounding close across
the windless air. The track turned right and ran
beside the fence. Liz kept on going straight
until she reached the creek. She stopped and looked
in front of her, at something that had caught
her eye. A rabbit's head was lying on
the ground, intact, the body simply gone.
A fox? thought Liz, or maybe even Miff?
She took a step and kicked the head into
the creek. It landed in cumbungi on
a mudbank near the other side. She walked
along the edge, alert for movement in
the water that might be a water-rat
or platypus. In all the times she'd come
down here she'd never seen a platypus.
They lived in there all right—Max said he got
them in his drumnet now and then—but they
were shy. Sometimes a water-rat would look
like one at first but then you'd see the white
tip on the tail. Wrong time of day, thought Liz.
She watched a pair of bubbles coming up
not far from where the mudbank disappeared
below the waterline. She used to think

they meant that something must be swimming there
but now she thought they were a kind of gas
escaping from the mud. She wandered on.
The wind was stirring now. Above the trees
a gang of magpies six or seven strong
was worrying a hawk. Their strategy
seemed well-rehearsed: while several niggled from
behind, a pair would climb above the hawk
and dive from different angles. Often one
or both would clip a tilting gilded wing
on their way through and send the hawk into
a brief unstable plunge. Its cries were shrill
but not alarmed. There was a feeling both
sides knew that this was mostly just for show.
The pageant disappeared behind the trees.
Liz high-stepped slowly through a stretch of thick
paspalum, looking out for snakes that might,
she was aware, already have emerged
from inside logs and under galvo sheets.
Back on more open ground she lobbed a lump
of quartz into the middle of the creek.
The splash was satisfying, and the rings
of water bobbing outwards were a sleight
of hand—you couldn't quite see how but as
you looked more rings kept on appearing from
the centre like a process speeded up.

Liz looked at bundles of dried rushes, sticks
and even logs wedged into tree forks high
above her head, a legacy of floods
from years before. She stood remembering
the transformations that had come through here,
the creek and all the lower paddocks gone,
and how the water would drain overnight
and leave the grass swept down and covered with
a skin of sifted mud. It always seemed
a kind of watershed: she missed it if
it didn't happen at least once a year.
The wind was stronger now. Dead leaves
were spinning off the branches, bits of bark
were being discarded from the red gum trunks.
Liz strolled along, her hands joined up beneath
her belly. 'Pew!' she said, and looked around.
The wind was suddenly directing smells
of rotting flesh at her, from where she'd been.
She must have walked right past it. Back she went.
A dozen steps and she was looking at
a decomposing ram, his belly ripped
wide open and his guts all emptied out.
Whose ram is this? And what on earth did that?
she wondered, standing over him upwind
so she at least was spared the primal stink.
The rumour that there was a panther round,

descended from some mascot cubs released
by US soldiers at the end of World
War Two, came back to her. Occasionally
the local paper ran a story on
some bovine carcass strangely disembowelled.
There'd be a picture of the farmer in
his gumboots, arms crossed, standing over it,
the story quoting him as saying things
like: I've been farming here for thirty years,
I swear I've never seen the likes of it.
The other story that'd get a go
was someone saying they'd been driving down
a back road late at night when suddenly
a panther ran across in front of them.
More likely it's a big black dog, thought Liz.
She left the carcass and continued down
a rabbit track that ran along the creek.
Across the other side a barbed-wire fence
between two properties was heaped with sticks,
dead grass and rushes from the floods so that
it looked more like a hedge. It ended with
a massive river red gum serving as
the strainer post. The wires around the trunk
had cut into the bark the way the strings
around a rolled roast cut into the fat.
Liz noticed that the cuts had bled a bit,

a ruby sap now crystallised in lines.
She wondered if the tree would get ringbarked
or if the bark would grow around the wire.
She thought about an afternoon spent on
her uncle's farm when she was seventeen,
her cousin showing off by hatcheting
a low down collar round a yellow-box,
how easy it had been to kill that tree.
Not far from where the strainer red gum stood
the creek went shallow for about ten yards
and in that writhing stretch you could make out
two broken lines of heavy rocks joined up
to form an awkward vee. Liz nearly smiled
remembering the first time that she'd seen
these rocks. Returning home she filled in Len
about the native fish-trap that she'd found,
the place where local Aborigines
had funnelled fish into a narrow pass
so they could catch them there. Len put her straight.
He'd made it with a mate of his, Pete Sharp,
one Christmas holidays when they were twelve.
He added that as far as he could tell
it didn't work. At that point Max had come
into the room and said his drumnet worked
and that a stick of dynamite was best.
Liz buttoned up her coat and left the track

to get a better look into the creek.
The wind had dropped but it was drizzling now.
The creek was wider here and looked quite deep.
Something was happening. The surface of
the water close to her was being disturbed
by semi-circles pulsing outwards from
the edge. They stopped. And started further down
the edge, about two yards away, and stopped
again, but not before Liz saw its back
of dark brown fur. A water-rat she thought.
A line of bubbles came up heading for
the middle, leading her attention on.
The bubbles stopped, and over near the far
side of the creek a platypus came up
and floated there, its duck bill looking like
a dark removable accessory.
Keep very still. Make like an old tree trunk,
Liz told herself, expecting that the show
would soon be over. But the platypus
remained. It kept as still as Liz for what
she thought were several minutes then it kind
of wiggled and was gone. Another line
of bubbles came up heading down the creek.
Liz quickly followed them along the bank.
The platypus appeared again. This time
before it dived it wiggled hard enough

to make a little splash. How cute! thought Liz.
A row of bubbles headed for the bank
across the other side. Liz waited for
the platypus to show itself again
but nothing happened. Minutes passed. Liz ran
her fingers through her hair. They came out wet.
She turned and headed back the way she'd come.
The drizzle shifted into steady rain,
reducing distant objects to a blur.
The trees were not much good as shelter now.
They turned the raindrops into bigger drops
and let them go. The creek was pelleted.
Between the fish-trap and the carcass Liz
decided she'd cut through the paddocks to
the house. It meant she'd have to climb a bull
fence on the way but it was worth it just
to get home earlier. She left the track
and headed out into the open space
of Len's ten acre barley crop. The green
monotony relaxed her mind. She walked
against the rain diagonally across
the paddock, leaving trampled barley in
her wake. What bloody hypocrites, she thought,
we'd give Amanda hell if she did this.
The bull fence looked impossible: too high,
with rows of tight barbed-wire along the top.

Liz put her hand around a barb of one
and squeezed until it nearly pierced her skin.
She thought of German prison camps and rolls
of spiky wire coiled out like broken springs
between the trenches in some footage of
the Western Front. Designed to go through skin.
Invented by a woman, Max had said.
That's just the sort of thing you'd say, thought Liz.
She noticed that the barbless bottom wires
were pretty loose. She got down on her back
and slid through like she'd seen a soldier do
in colour footage from another war.
Her oilskin coat got muddied and the rain
was blinding in her upturned face but she
enjoyed the physicality of it.
She walked across the empty paddock to
the corner where the gate was fastened shut
with orange baling twine tied in a bow.
The lane from there went down towards the yard
and entered it between the kennels and
the far machinery shed. Behind that shed
was where a generation's worth of old
machinery had been ditched: old ploughs, old discs,
an early header that was vaguely like
an oversize piano on three wheels.
The grass was never cut in there. It was

a small forgotten place. Liz glanced at it
as she went trudging past. Sometimes in spring
she'd used it as a spot where she could grow
a few unnoticed marijuana plants.
Len smoked a joint with her occasionally
but over time had grown less interested.
Max might have seen a few strange weeds in there
but Liz was confident he wouldn't have
a clue. His knowledge of the natural world
was not as detailed as you would expect
from one who'd spent his whole life in the bush.
He knew a lot about the land round here
but Liz had found herself correcting him
on things like bird calls, clouds and native shrubs.
She knew he'd say, if someone challenged him,
he'd been too busy working all his life.
The rain was getting fast and noisy now.
It scoured the galvo roofs. The near and far
machinery sheds were gutterless. The rain
slid out and frayed from each small channel like
so many hoses running all at once.
It brimmed along the gutters on the house,
an upheld stream, and poured into the tank
with noises from the filling of a bath.
It caused a million tiny movements on
the dirt in front of Liz, an insect plague

too quick and uniform for her to see.
And in the centre of the yard it dripped
and trickled from the bumper bars and mud
flaps of a station wagon that she'd seen
before: the fella with the funny name.
She nodded to him as she stepped inside.
He nodded back and said, 'Hello again'.
Beside him at the table Max and Len
were sitting both with pamphlets in their hands.
A thicker booklet lay in front of Len.
Its title was *How Jews Control the Banks*.
'Ya soaked', said Len. 'Yep. It was fun!' said Liz.
Max looked at her as if she were a twit.
'Some homework for a rainy day, eh Pop?'
said Liz, returning his unpleasant stare.
He looked away. 'Just finishing', said Len.
Their thin-lipped visitor, whose accent Liz
decided sounded slightly Dutch or Boer,
stood up and said, 'Could I just use your phone?'.
'It's been cut off', said Len. Liz felt herself
becoming cold. 'I'm gonna have a shower',
she said, and went into the laundry where
the recess was. Before she closed the door
she heard the stranger calling after her:
'At least no-one can cut the water off!'
She stripped away her clothes and stepped into

a concentrated downpour warmer than
her blood. The pleasure weakened her at once.
It spread out through her heavy body like
the irresistible effect of dope.
She felt like sitting down. She stood a while
and then gave in. The water softened her.
It beat a kind of numbness into her,
especially on her neck and shoulders where
it mostly fell. She stayed quite still like that
until the temperature began to drop.
Out in the kitchen Len was sitting with
his pamphlet rolled up tightly in his hands.
The other man and Max had disappeared.
'Learn anything?' said Liz, still dripping, with
her belly showing through her undone robe.
'Few things', said Len. 'They gonna get our farm
back for us then?' said Liz. She tried to do
her robe up but the two sides wouldn't meet.
Len said, 'They got a fighting fund. They say . . .'.
Liz cut him off, 'In other words they're not!'.
Len dropped the pamphlet on the table where
it sprang half-open, rolled a bit then stopped.
'They can arrange publicity', he said.
Liz started walking down the hall. 'You say
some pretty stupid things', she said. 'Like what?'
yelled Len. Liz stuck her head into the lounge

room where Amanda had the telly on.
'Like what?' yelled Len. 'You bloody know!'
yelled Liz.
She went into the bedroom, shed her robe
and started getting dressed. 'I bloody don't!'
yelled Len. She stretched a track suit on and went
into the kitchen. 'Gonna go to town',
Len mumbled, standing up. 'Get these', said Liz.
Amongst the notices on Len's pin board
there was a shopping list for rice, flour, yeast,
detergent, bacon, salt and foil. She tore
it off and slapped it down in front of him.
'And what's in town?' she added, walking to
the sink. 'The footy club, that's what', said Len.
Liz filled the kettle, put it on the stove
and said, 'The footy finished weeks ago'.
'Well, it's a kinda social club', said Len
Liz stared at him. 'Don't gimme that!' she sneered,
'It's just somewhere for little boys to get
half-pissed and watched their porno videos!'
Before she'd finished speaking Len had turned
his back on her and wrenched the sliding door.
The rain was roaring on the galvo roofs.
He stepped outside, and with his head tipped down.
ran over to the near machinery shed
where Max's truck was parked. Liz shut the door

and turned around to see Amanda there.
'It's really heavy, Mum', she said. 'Sure is.
Looks like it's gonna settle in', said Liz.
She looked a moment at the range then swung
the fire box door. The tray below the grate
was full of ash as fine as sifted flour.
A cardboard box beside the range was filled
with kindling and some lengths of yellow-box.
She looked for paper. Seeing none she took
the telephone directory off the bench
and started ripping 'Information' out,
then 'Local Government' and half of 'A'.
She made a bed of screwed-up pages on
the grate, poked in the kindling and some wood
and lit the bottom layer with a match.
It smoked and paused and hardly took at all.
Liz marched into the laundry, grabbed her hair
drier, came back and plugged it in beside
the phone. She aimed the nozzle at the grate
and switched the drier on. There was a small
jet whine, a breath of smoke and ash was swirled
back into Liz's face, and in the fire
box things began to blaze immediately.

CHAPTER SIX

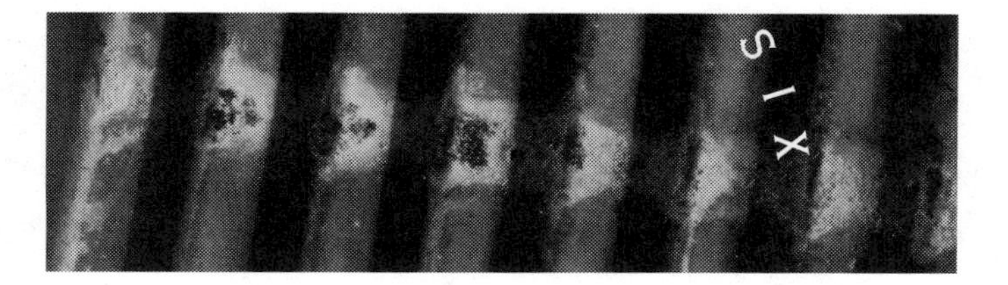

FOR NAUSEA—ONE TABLET TWICE A DAY.
Liz read the warnings further down the pack
and then the unpronounceable brand-name.
She popped a yellow tablet through its foil
and placed it on her tongue and swallowed hard.
Outside the heavy cloud was breaking up.
Enormous polished shapes of pale blue, flat
and hard as porcelain were visible.
The rain had stopped around daybreak but Liz
still listened to it in her mind. She felt
its threshing on the corrugated iron
had made her stay awake for half the night.
The sound of it had simply been too loud.
The yard and all the paddocks Liz could see
from where she stood against the sliding door
were also covered with new shiny shapes,
great pools and sheets of water everywhere.
So this is what three inches and a bit
looks like, thought Liz, converting what the gauge
had said into a figure that made sense.
No single downpour through the winter months
had dumped as much as this. The creek would be
in flood. The tank was overflowing still,
a breeze-bent trickle from the exit spout.
There was a constant background noise of frogs.
Liz fixed herself some instant coffee in

a mug and accidentally tipped in too
much milk, which made it look like liquid clay.
She stood back up against the sliding door
and looked at aspects of the new regime.
The house's emptiness was comforting.
The other three had gone off in the ute
with Max and Len still bickering about
an offer on the herd. Max felt they should
hold out for more. I dunno why he needs
to swear so much, thought Liz, especially with
Amanda there. She poured three-quarters of
her milk luke-warm coffee down the sink.
Things wouldn't be so tense if Max could stop
being such a grumpy prick. What made him act
like that? Apparently he had a lot
of lower back pain from an episode
when he was in his teens. A bulling cow
had mounted him and wrecked his lower discs.
Len said the pain was constant and at times
it got unbearable. Of course it would
affect your mood, thought Liz. She noted Max
had never mentioned it in front of her.
Too proud? Perhaps. But back pain by itself
was not the key to Max's character.
He would have been exactly like he is
without the injury, decided Liz.

And what about Amanda's attitude?
What stupid crap had Len been telling her?
There wasn't any point in fighting back.
Not now. However far you raised the stakes
the other side could always raise them more.
She slumped a bit against the steady door,
remembering a story that she'd read
about a farmer at Katandra West.
He was a dairy farmer, though he kept
some bees as well. He'd borrowed to expand
and finished up by going broke instead.
He'd stood his hives across the only gate
into his farm, and when the Sheriffs came
to turf him out he'd stand there with his gun
and fire a shot, which made the bees go mad.
They'd swarm and form a natural barrier.
The story had a photo of him with
his shotgun, standing tall behind the hives.
But it was just to get publicity,
thought Liz, he knew he couldn't keep them beat.
She reached a glass down off the shelf above
the sink and filled it full. She didn't feel
like drinking it but Len had said it was
important that you keep your fluids up.
Essential juices, was his silly phrase.
She looked into the glass. It swarmed with specks.

The force of all the constant funnelled rain
into the tank had stirred the sediment.
She held the glass towards the light and looked
again. One speck could be identified
as half a little shiny insect husk,
another few were legs, the rest were too
minute to pick. Liz stared. They swirled like some
great flock of birds observed from far away.
No thanks. She tipped them down the sink, pulled out
her unused handkerchief and stood the glass
below the tap. She laid the handkerchief
across the glass's rim so you could see
its shape, and with her finger poked a small
depression there. She used her other hand
to turn the tap on to a gentle stream,
which slowly filled the glass. A tiny mound
of dead flea dots collected in the cloth,
a bit like straining very fine tea leaves.
Liz held the glass towards the light again.
The water didn't look entirely pure
but it would do. She tipped it down her throat
and felt it sliding through her nausea.
How long before the tablet did its thing?
She propped back up against the sliding door.
The thought of checking out the creek in flood
took hold of her. The walk she'd had along

there yesterday had been a pleasant change
and hadn't made her stomach any worse.
She grabbed the same oilskin and stepped outside.
Waist-high to her, along a weatherboard
beside the door, there was a wooden rail
held up by metal saddles like the ones
that hold up curtain rods. This rail had been
installed by Len about a year ago.
You put your gumboots upside-down in there,
which stopped the rain and mice from getting in,
although it didn't solve the problem of
the other group of opportunists that
you sometimes found in them. Most days the rail
was chock-a-block with long-necked rubber boots
but only Liz's pair remained today.
She slid them out and shook them upside-down
with no result. Not satisfied she ducked
inside and found a can of Insect Rid
and sprayed the stuff into her boots and shook
them upside-down again. This time a small
dark ball rolled out. Liz squatted down and looked
at it: a Red-Back Spider with its legs
curled up around its body, quivering.
It clenched. She stood and squashed it with her foot.
A hint of Insect Rid persisted in
the air. It irritated Liz's nose.

She rummaged through her pockets looking for
her handkerchief and then remembered it
was lying wet and useless in the sink.
She cleared her nose, one wheezy nostril at
a time like Max and Len, kicked off her shoes,
threw them inside and put her gumboots on.
The walk across the yard went zig-zag as
she sought the biggest puddles to enjoy.
Her gumboots made her feel less vulnerable.
She paused a minute at the other side
to pat the dogs, a pair of Queensland blues,
and then decided they could come with her.
She let them off and started down the lane
she'd taken yesterday, expecting them
to follow her. Instead they raced away
along the other lane, the one the ute
had taken earlier, and disappeared.
Not much in those two heads, thought Liz. A group
of magpies watched her from the nearby fence.
They seemed subdued, as if the heavy rain
had worn them out. The lane was patched with big
brown puddles, varied in their shapes as lakes.
Liz marched through each of them in turn, not sad
to be behaving like a twelve-year-old.
The gate before the creek was still pushed back
but on the ground the perfect arc had gone,

replaced by wrinkles indicating that
the rain had fallen hard enough to run.
Liz looked with pleasure at the scene beyond,
imagining the places that she'd walked
in yesterday, which now were overcome
by one enormous clumsy sliding force.
She sniffed the flat sour smell of churned-up mud.
The water was a kind of milky brown.
It covered lavish curving areas
both sides of where the usual creek had been.
A gothic tongue of it extended right
across the middle of the barley crop.
It shows you where the low bits are, thought Liz.
She stepped into the swirling edge of it.
The waterline was halfway up her boots.
A trembling lip appeared on each, right there,
the current side, the way that bigger lips
were clinging to the tree trunks further out.
She took some stirring steps until her boots
were only several inches from being filled
and then retreated to the edge again.
The water must have reached its highest mark
at least a few hours earlier because
a carefully assembled line of sticks
and twigs and bark and rushes ran beside
the present edge a yard or so away

in wavy parallel. Liz used her foot
to scrape the only opening in this line,
remembering a film she'd seen about
a flood in Holland where a dyke was breached.
She started walking, led on by the line.
The thin-skinned water, pushing in the same
direction held a kind of narrative:
connected things were always happening.
Liz stopped. The feeling something wasn't right
had been gestating in her mind a while
and now she knew exactly what it was.
Her foot was wet. The left one. Very wet.
These gumboots weren't so brilliant after all.
She stepped into the water just to see
if she could fell it getting any worse
and stood there. No. It mustn't be too bad.
She came back out and slowly walked along
the edge as if it needed pressing down.
Small pouring noises seemed to come from near
and far. Occasionally there was a splash,
which Liz assumed would be a falling branch.
In little coves she noticed heaped-up scum
as dirty curly as the wool on sheep.
Out in the shifting middle forks of trees
at surface height collected clumps of sticks,
each one untidy as an eagle's nest.

At places where a group of trees was close
enough together, bobbing islands made
of logs and sticks and reeds and bark were stuck.
On one of these a willy-wagtail hopped
about the way you see them hop about
on cows: to find a treat, to ride the bumps.
Liz wondered how the platypus had coped.
She waded through a separate pool that must
have filled when things were at their broadest reach,
and joined a rabbit track that started from
the other side and led to higher ground.
Her boot felt worse. It squelched. She pulled it off
and emptied out a cupful of the flood.
The track went round a giant red gum, one
that Len had reckoned went back well before
the whities got into this area.
It had deposited a crunchy floor
of sticks, dead leaves and curled-up bits of bark.
Liz sauntered over it, remembering
another reason why these boots were good.
Last summer, wearing shorts and thongs, she'd come
through here and put her foot down close beside
the one soft stick, the one that moved, the one
that straightened out, the one that disappeared.
The Common Eastern Brown: apparently
its venom was among the strongest in

the world. Liz hated snakes, and couldn't see
why Max and Len were unafraid of them.
Len said they'd rather run away than fight.
She'd once seen Max extract one from a log
the way he pulled the rope to start the pump,
then crack its head off in one movement like
the action that you'd use to hurl a stone.
Liz frowned. The thought of them was bad enough.
She looked down at the creek, at something that
had caught her eye, a different sort of shape.
The bloated carcass of a Hereford
was rolling through the middle, dipping so
you only saw its underbelly and
its waving legs, then surfacing enough
for you to see the flanks and maybe glimpse
the lolling head. It looked as if it must
have died a while ago: the fur was worn
away in places and the tail was gone.
It looked like it would stink despite the cold.
Liz watched its progress, wondering if it
was one of theirs, if any of the herd
had been that far upstream in recent times.
It bumped into some branches, dithered for
a moment then spun free and carried on
its journey only to get jammed between
two further branches meeting in a fork.

The image of the cow still wedged up there
tomorrow when the waterline had dropped
intruded into Liz's mind and stuck.
It would be worth another walk to see
a sight like that, so morbid and surreal.
She stood there trying to imagine what
might happen once the flood support was gone.
The pregnant shape seemed balanced well enough
but would it topple once the belly lost
that putrid gas? You couldn't really say.
The sodden body of a rabbit lay
beside the track. Liz guessed it must have drowned.
The flood was just like fire, she thought, it drove
things out, consuming some of them itself
and forcing others into places where
their nemeses could get a grip on them.
One time the creek had been in flood she'd come
to watch it with Amanda and they'd seen
a kookaburra landing in a tree
with something like a bootlace in its beak.
Amanda thought it was a baby snake
but Liz had put her straight: the ones that size
were mostly legless lizards, pretty much
the same except they didn't have forked tongues
and did have two small tell-tale holes for ears.
She started following the track again,

remembering an incident from years
ago when they were still at Nan and Pop's.
She'd been collecting ripe tomatoes in
the vegie patch and just as she stood up
Len dropped a legless lizard down the front
of her loose shirt. She'd slapped him on the face
more out of fright than anger, though she told
him afterwards she'd just been mad at him.
He'd never played a trick like that again.
Deciding that she'd had enough, she turned
and walked back down the track until she got
to where the body of the rabbit lay,
where something made her stop. It wasn't dead.
Its swollen eyes were slightly open and
its head was nodding with each rapid breath,
as if it had collapsed into a trance.
Liz stared. It obviously was going to die
but maybe she should kill it now to end
the suffering. It wasn't hard to do.
She'd often been around when Len killed one.
You simply held the head down with your foot
and tugged the back legs so the spinal cord
got disconnected from the brain. A cinch.
She stood there undecided and subdued.

CHAPTER SEVEN

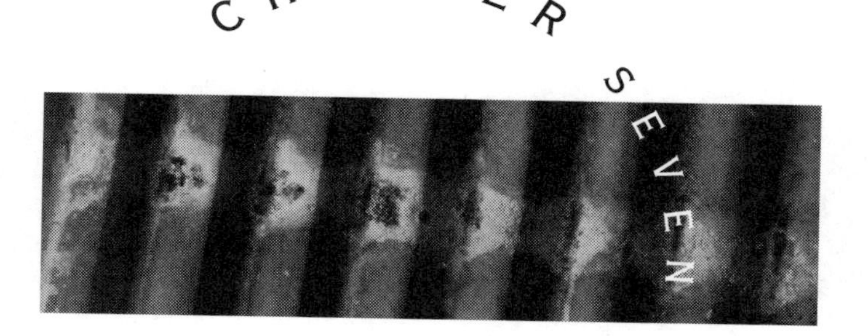

THE WOODEN STOCKYARD RAILS HAD BEEN REPLACED.
Len thought of all the times he'd perched up on
the highest rail with other children like
a row of jockeys waiting for a start
while in the yard dense herds of cattle droned.
He still could feel the smoothness of the rails,
how they'd been oiled and polished by the years
of bovine pushing that they'd stood against,
and how the cracks were packed with greasy hairs.
He'd often found himself caressing those
worn surfaces while he was leaning there.
And now the rails were gone because the wood
could harbour stock disease, apparently.
The Council had condemned them late last year.
Len leaned against the metal rails and watched
a welder working on the other side,
about a good-sized footy field away.
The welding rod was tapped a few times on
a metal post, there was a sizzling flash
and Len stopped watching, to protect his eyes.
He ran his finger down the junction of
a post and rail, along the blistered slag
of someone's shoddy weld. The underneath
was mostly just a jagged hollow where
the arc had melted through. Ya shoulda screwed
her down a bit, thought Len, some kid'll cut

his fingers there. He turned and looked across
the road at D.G. FARRELL FARM SUPPLIES
SUB-AGENT FOR DALGETY REAL ESTATE.
A smaller sign below said LIVESTOCK SALES.
He peered through plate glass at the silhouettes
of customers for any sign of Max
who'd gone in there an hour or so ago
to see old Farrell on his offer on
the Herefords. 'Stay there, I won't be long',
he'd said before he'd slammed the driver's door.
Like I was just a kid or even just
a bloody dog, thought Len. He crossed the road
and went into the store. Long rows of shelves
stacked high with useful things confronted him.
He went up to the counter and explained
who he was looking for. 'He's with the boss',
said someone in a dustcoat, pointing to
a louvred window in a wall behind
the open office space. Len saw the tops
of two heads bobbing there and heard a snatch
of cursing laughter, which he recognised
as Max's mixed in with another man's.
He wandered back along the rows of shelves
examining the products, some of which
he understood while others drew a blank.
A woman in a pair of overalls

walked past him with a steel-jawed rabbit trap
held casually between a finger and
a thumb. Its little silver chain and peg
and shiny zig-zag lines gave it a look
of some bizarre key-ring accessory.
He found himself in front of HERBICIDES.
Bright tins and plastic drums of it were stacked
together in a pleasing symmetry.
Most brands had labels with a cheerful blurb
that said how excellent the contents were,
and underneath the blurb, in smaller print,
there'd be a list of warnings starting with
the usual one: AVOID CONTACT WITH SKIN.
Len read the label on a brand they'd used
a while ago to knock down Broad-Leaved Dock,
and thought indignantly how Max had been,
as always, cavalier by emptying
the tin into a drum of water where
he stirred them up together with his arm.
The store was suddenly resounding with
a crackling two-stroke snarl as someone pulled
a demonstration chainsaw into life
and revved it for a bit then let it die.
Len registered how much the spray now cost
and wondered if it would be worth a go
at what his uncle recommended once—

stop using everything: the herbicides,
the pesticides, the fertilisers and
the drench, and see if what you saved was more
than all the lost production that you copped.
Another shot of brazen laughter came
out of the boss's office followed by
a kind of double clanging sound, which Len
immediately suspected was the sound
of empty tinnies getting dropped into
an empty metal bin. The office door
swung back and Max and old man Farrell walked
into the store still chuckling over what
had just been said. Max left the other man
behind the counter, walked past Len without
a word and headed over to the ute.
Len followed at a distance, wondering
how many tinnies Max had drunk in there.
The sun was pretty close to setting now.
Its fire was easier to look at than
the welder's bluish flare across the yards.
Len got into the ute. 'So, any news?'
he asked. 'He's droppin' out tomorrow for
another look', said Max. They drove through town
in silence. At the derestriction sign
Len asked what chance there was that Farrell might
increase his offer on the Herefords.

'More fuckin' chance than if I'd left it up
to you', said Max, accelerating hard.
They let themselves go back to wordlessness.
Out through the right hand window now the sun
was down among the trees, revealing how
much dust and smoke were hanging in the air.
It seemed more like high summer than mid spring.
There must have been a farmer burning off.
They passed the ruins of a shearing shed
where Len remembered playing hide-and-seek
with several other kids when he was small.
The shed had been in operation then
and all the yards were crammed with bulging sheep.
The running boards were coated with the shit
and piss of those who'd been reduced that day
and Len had slipped and gashed his forearm on
a rusty nail protruding from a stud.
He ran his finger up and down the scar,
a little pale smooth worm that never changed,
and looked back at the shed. A lot of sheets
of iron had fallen off and other sheets
were hanging loose and curling like the bark
on red gums does when it's half through being shed.
They didn't see another vehicle
until a semi passed them carrying
three tiers of pigs. High up a head was jammed

sideways between two outside rails so one
pink ear was flapping in the turbulence.
In other places legs were sticking out.
Max switched his parkers and his blinkers on
and left the bitumen and turned into
the gravel road that led down to the farms.
The cabin noise increased dramatically.
Len went to speak then closed his mouth again,
compelled to silence by the roaring road.
He waited till the ute was stopping in
the yard, then asked, 'What time's he coming out?'.
''Bout eight', said Max. 'That's not a lotta time
to get the steers', said Len, and waited for
his father to respond. Max didn't say
a word. He sat there staring straight ahead,
a taxi driver waiting for a fare.
Len didn't try again. He got out of
the ute and watched it turn and drive away.
The dogs came running up to him, a pair
of cheerful idiots. They sniffed his boots
and trouserlegs excitedly, as if
they'd never come across such things before.
He walked towards the house, then noticed that
the lights weren't on, assumed the other two
were still outside and did a quick skirt round
the garden and the sheds. No sign of them.

They must be down the creek, he thought,
   and stepped
inside. The kitchen had cooled down. He put
his hand against the fire box door. Dead cold.
He went into their bedroom where he found
their cupboard open, Liz's clothes all gone
and on the floor a nearly empty pack
of Jumbo Garbage Bags. He went into
Amanda's room and found her cupboard had
been emptied too. He felt the same as when
his flat had been done over years ago
in Adelaide, though this was tidier.
Amanda's room had suddenly grown dark.
How long had he been blankly standing there?
He turned on several lights and went outside
where there was still a residue of day.
The air was cooling. Down the creek he heard
some kookaburras laughing raucously.
A dog's nose pressed into his trouserleg.
He clicked his fingers twice and walked across
the yard to where the forty-fours were still
just visible. The dogs stayed close to him.
Arriving there he chained them up as much
by feel as sight, and heard the brushy beat
of one dog's wagging tail against its drum.
He started back towards the empty house,

remembering the story of the time
his uncle sawed his thumb off benching wood.
Apparently he kept on going till
the trailer load was done, chained up his dogs
and only then drove into town, the thumb
beside him on the seat, blood everywhere.
It's funny how a person will behave
like that, quite normally, when they're in shock.

CHAPTER

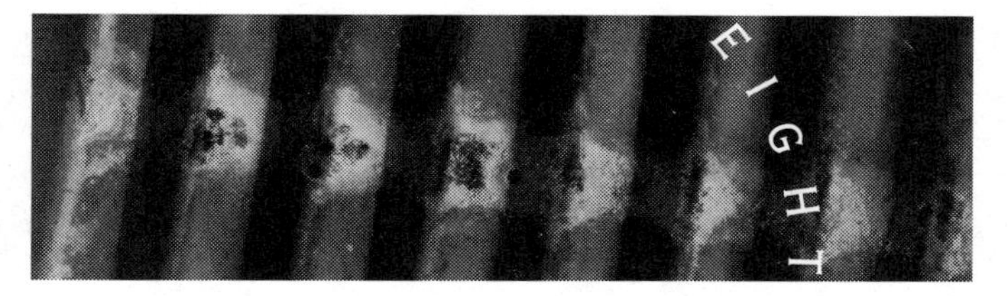

JOE BLAKE, THOUGHT MAX, THE FIRST ONE FOR THE YEAR.
He was already half way down the hall
before he'd registered the meaning of
that sound, that quiet sliding sound behind
the pile of boxes in the children's room.
It was just chance he'd gone in there at all.
He hardly ever went in there these days.
The room was mostly used for storing stuff:
old bed frames, other furniture, and in
one corner many cardboard boxes full
of bottles, magazines and papers stacked
four wide, three deep and over six foot high.
He'd only gone in there to resupply
himself with paper as his usual store
of it beside the stove was finished now.
He walked into the kitchen with a box
of copies of *The Sun* and *Weekly Times*
and put it down beside the empty one
and wondered what to do about the snake.
Few years since one came in the house, he thought.
He had a pot of boiled potatoes on
the stove, which he was heating up again,
and next to that some lamb chops in a pan.
He took a handle in each hand and steered
towards the table where he put them down.
The chops were lying in a pool of fat.

Outside, the sun was gone completely now
with just a shrinking pink and purple arc
to show where it had been, the strongest stars
were showing through, and frogs had come alive.
Max stepped out onto the verandah, looked
a moment at the setting dark and picked
his torch up off a chair beside the door.
He went into the children's room again
and looked at where he thought the noise had been.
Beside the pile of boxes was a chest
of drawers and in between the two there was
a one inch gap held shadowed by the room's
bare bulb. Max poked the torchlight there and saw
a section of the dark brown skirting board
and parallel to that, in lighter brown,
a fine-clad segment of the snake, quite thick.
Six foot for sure, thought Max. He wondered which
direction it was lying in. And there,
it shifted, but he couldn't tell which way.
His eyesight wasn't what it used to be
but more than that the scaly pattern seemed
to flow both ways at once. It was the same
effect as when two lengths of chain were close
together running from a pulley wheel.
It moved again, and kept on moving so
this time Max saw that it was heading left.

He quickly got down on his hands and knees
and forced his arm into the widening gap
then got his shoulder in beside the chest
of drawers and pushed it even further back
while feeling with his fingers for the snake.
But all he handled was the skirting board.
'You prick', he whispered, getting to his feet.
He put his hip against the chest of drawers
and pushed it sideways so the gap was now
about six foot, and shone the torchlight in
behind the pile of boxes where he saw
a mass of dusty sagging spider webs
so thick it seemed like fog: the more intense
the light you shine on it, the less you see.
He wandered back into the kitchen, paused
and shut the door, revealing two straight things,
a double barrel shotgun and a broom.
And while he stood there voices came to him.
He glanced up at the wireless on the shelf
beside his head and saw that it was on,
but with the sound as low as it would go
so someone had to be that close to hear.
And even then it seemed subliminal,
like one of Len's attempts to give the smokes
away, a quiet tape he'd played at night.
Max switched the wireless off and stared at what

was in the corner just in front of him.
He reached and took the longer of the two,
the broom, and went back to the children's room,
and brusquely poked the handle in between
the pile of boxes and the wall. It made
a scraping sound, half muffled by the webs.
He waved it down then up so all the stuff
was torn away and came out clinging to
the handle like the pale decayed remains
of nylon stockings from another age.
The torchlight showed no snake. He went round to
the other wall and did the same thing there.
Again the torchlight showed the snake had gone.
Max focused on the boxes, thinking that
it might have slid somewhere in there, the way
that snakes slide up between the bales in stacks
of hay. He thought of how, when he was young,
he would have pulled a stack to bits for one
but now he wouldn't even bother with
a little stack like this—five minutes' work.
He knew it wasn't just his wretched back
or laziness, but how he saw things now.
No bloody point, he thought, it might hang round
here for a day or two but it'll go.
He took the torch and broom back with him to
the kitchen, set them down and checked his food.

Just warm. Around the pool of fat there was
a rim of paleness where the shallow edge
had started to congeal. He got a plate
and occupied about one half of it
with dripping chops, and filled in nearly all
the other half with low potato mounds
then coloured in the wedge of space still left
with several shakes of plush tomato sauce.
He sat down with his knife and fork, and ate.
The house was still. There was a crackle in
the fire box now and then, the random pop
of cooling roofing iron, and not much else.
Max scooped a forkful of potato through
the sauce and listened for that other sound.